April Fool!

by
Karen
Gray
Ruelle

Holiday House / New York

With lots of love to Mom and Dad,
who taught me how important
it is to have fun

Library of Congress Cataloging-in-Publication Data
Ruelle, Karen Gray.
April fool! / Karen Gray Ruelle.—1st ed.
p. cm.
Summary: Harry, his little sister, Emily, and their parents all play tricks
on each other for April Fools' Day.
ISBN 0-8234-1686-0 (hardcover)
[1. April Fools' Day—Fiction. 2. Brothers and sisters—Fiction.] I. Title.

PZ7.R88525 Ap 2002
[E]—dc21 2001024485

Contents

1. April Fools' Day

Harry came home from school.
Then he got a snack.
Snacks helped him to think
of good ideas.
His little sister, Emily, got a snack, too.
"Sunday is the most important day
of the year," he told her.
"My birthday?" asked Emily.
"No. Sunday is April Fools' Day,"
said Harry.
"We have to think of tricks to play
on Mom and Dad."

"Why?" said Emily.

"Because it is fun," said Harry.

"And because I know you are tricky.

I already have some tricks.

You have to think of some, too.

Sunday is only two days away."

Harry and Emily thought about tricks.

They ate some cookies.

They thought some more.

They ate some grapes.

"Do you remember last year?"
asked Emily.

"We put toy spiders in Mom's coffee.
   She was very surprised.
   Let's do that again."
"It will not work," said Harry.
"It has to be a new trick.
   That is a trick for little kids."
They thought some more.
They thought until
   all the snacks were gone.

"Remember that trick we played
  on Dad?" asked Emily.
"We put a whoopee cushion
  on his chair.
  It made a funny, loud noise.
  He was so surprised.
  Let's do that again."

"It will not work," said Harry.

"He knows that old trick.

It has to be a new trick.

It has to be a real surprise."

"I know," said Emily.

"I can play

a trick on you."

"If you tell me about it,

it will not work," said Harry.

"It will not be a surprise."

"Then I will not tell you," said Emily.

"Do not use a toy spider

or a whoopee cushion.

It will not be a surprise," said Harry.

"Oh, you will be surprised," said Emily.

"I am very tricky."

2. Tricky Tricks

It was the day
before April
Fools' Day.
All morning,
Emily practiced
tricks.

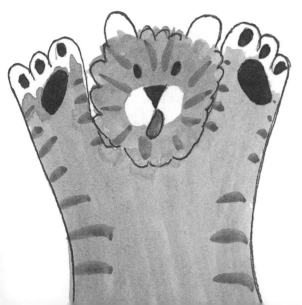

She jumped
out from
behind a chair.
"Boo!" said Emily.

"You did not surprise me," said Harry.
"You need a better trick."
  Emily made a scared face.
  She said to Harry,
"Look out behind you!"
"I know there is nothing there,"
  said Harry. "To trick me,
  you will need a big surprise.
  The bigger the surprise,
  the better the trick."
  After lunch, Harry and Emily
  went to the magic shop.
  They brought all the money
  from their piggy banks,
  just in case.

There were lots of tricky surprise things
at the magic shop.
There were decks
of disappearing cards.
There were amazing trick handkerchiefs.
There were silly masks
and squirting coins.
There were floppy forks and knives.

There were also plastic spiders
and whoopee cushions.

"We don't need those," said Harry.
"We already have some at home.
  Besides, we won't use them this year."
  Emily found something she liked.
  Harry found something, too.
  They had just enough money
  from their piggy banks.

3. The Big Day

"Wake up, Emily!" said Harry.

"Look at all the snow!"

"Where? Where?" said Emily.

She looked out the window.

It was sunny and bright.

There was no snow at all.

"April Fool!" said Harry.

It was April Fools' Day at last!

"Time for breakfast,"
   said Harry and Emily's mother.
"Hurry up or your ice cream will melt,"
   said their father.
"Ice cream for breakfast?" said Harry.
"Yum!" said Emily.
"April Fool!"
   said their mother and father.

Later, Harry set
the table for lunch.
He put a jar of nuts
on the table.
"Dad, can you
open this?
It is stuck," he said.

His father
unscrewed the lid.
Out jumped
a toy snake!
"April Fool!"
said Harry.

At lunch, Harry said to his mother,
"Aren't you going to answer the door?"
"I didn't hear the doorbell," she said.
"It just rang," said Harry.
"Oh," said his mother.

She went to the door.

Nobody was there.

"April Fool!" said Harry.

Harry's April Fools' Day tricks
were a great success.

He had tricked everyone.

His parents had tricked

him and Emily.

But Emily had not played any tricks.

All afternoon, Harry was ready.

He checked behind every door.

Emily was never there.

When he read his book,

he made sure

there was nothing

hiding in it.

But Emily had no tricks

for Harry.

Maybe she was too little

to play a good trick.

4. The Last Laugh

Harry and Emily went out to play.
When they came back, Emily was
hiding something behind her back.
She went to her mother and said,
"Look what I found! Can I keep it?"
She pulled out a stiff leash
with no pet in it.
She jiggled it.
It looked like an invisible pet
was pulling at it.

"What is that?" asked her mother.

"April Fool!" said Emily.

"You are very tricky,"
said her mother.

"I hope you have a better
trick for me," said Harry.

Their father was in the kitchen.

Emily went in and said,

"Look at my new pet."

She jiggled the leash again.

"What kind of pet is that?"
asked her father.

"April Fool! It's an April Fool pet!"
said Emily.

"Very tricky, Emily," said her father.

Harry waited for his trick from Emily.

There were no tricks at dinner.

There were no tricks at story time.

There were no tricks at bath time.

There were no tricks at all.

Harry was disappointed.

"April Fools' Day is almost over,"
  said Harry.
"I'm surprised.
  You have not played
  a trick on me yet."
  Emily laughed.
"Did you say you are surprised?"
  she said. "April Fool!
  You said I could not surprise you.
  But I did. I surprised you
  by NOT playing a trick on you."
"You are really tricky, Emily,"
  said Harry.
"But that is not
  a real April Fools' Day trick."

Then Harry put on his slippers.

"ACK!" he shouted.

A toy spider fell out of each one.

"April Fool!" said Emily.

Then Harry sat down on his bed.
It made a funny, loud noise.
"April Fool!" said Emily.
"I surprised you again," she said.
"I am the trickiest sister
in the world!"
"You are tricky after all,"
said Harry.
"You even surprised me with
toy spiders and a whoopee cushion."

"Maybe next year,
   I can help you think of
   some more good tricks," said Emily.
"Okay," said Harry.
"I can think of some good tricks
   right now," said Emily.